A Kwame Nyong'o book

© 2006 Kwame Nyong'o

Published by Apes in Space Limited. This 3rd edition, 2018.

ISBN: 978-1482532173

A Tasty Maandazi

Written and Illustrated by
Kwame Nyong'o

For my mother, Jean Turkish, who always encouraged me to draw.

And a very special thanks to Alan Schroeder, Norman Green, David Ball, Olivier Lechien, Ebba Kalondo and Sophie Awour, for all their support without which this book would not have been possible.

Musa woke up to the familiar sound of roosters, one bright morning in Kenya. He and his family lived in a small village that sat upon the beautiful African coast. It was a place that was always warm and sunny.

"It is Saturday! It is going to be a fantastic day!" Musa said to himself as he grabbed his favourite T-shirt. "First thing I'll do is go to Mama Milka's to get one of her fresh, tasty *maandazis*! It would be so nice to have one right now!"

"Don't leave before taking tea, Musa," said Mother, as she poured little sister Shani's cup.

Musa gulped his tea, and then set out into the warm breeze toward Mama Milka's shop. She was quite a generous lady and had given Musa free *maandazis* many times before.

"*Jambo*," Musa greeted the large lady. "May I have a *maandazi*, please?" he asked, excited by the wonderful smell of ginger and cinnamon.

Mama lifted her head from the white dough that she was busy rolling. "Musa," she said with a sigh, "how many times have I given you a *maandazi* for free? It has been many, many times. From now on, you must pay three shillings for them."

"Three shillings?" Musa cried.

"Yes, and that is cheap. I charge the adults five shillings! Now go off and don't return unless you have some money. Musa, remember, you are a big boy these days. I know you can find a way to earn a little money." With that, Mama Milka returned to making her *maandazi* dough.

Disappointed, Musa wondered what to do. "I know!" he thought. "Mum can give me some money!" He bolted home to see Mother, whom he found bent over a bucket, washing the laundry in the courtyard.

"Mum, please give me three shillings so I can buy a *maandazi* from Mama Milka," Musa pleaded.

With a groan, Mother straightened up. "Musa, I don't have money for *maandazis* now. If you are feeling hungry, take a banana." She pointed toward the kitchen.

"But Mummy," Musa whined, "I'm tired of eating bananas. I want *maandazi*!"

Mother looked at him crossly, "Musa, if you want *maandazi*, you'll have to go out and make the money yourself! Now, no more begging." Mother returned to her washing.

"Humph!" Musa grunted and went to look for his father.

Musa found Father busy working at the wood carver's co-op. He liked the sound that the carvers made, "chip, chip, chip." The smell of freshly cut wood filled the air.

"*Baba*, please give me three shillings so that I can buy a *maandazi*. I'm so hungry and I want to eat one," he said, rubbing his tummy with enthusiasm.

"My son," Father replied, looking up from the lion that he was carving, "you know very well that I do not have money for treats like *maandazis*. The money that I make must be used for clothes and school fees. Go and eat fruits at home."

"Oh, please, *Baba*?" Musa begged.

"No, no," Father refused. "Now go away and don't bother me; I am very busy here."

Musa wandered home feeling quite unhappy. He found little sister Shani playing with some toys out front and told her all that had happened.

"*Lakini* Musa, people at school have always said that you draw well. Maybe you can draw and sell some pictures for our neighbours?" She pointed toward the pencil and pad of paper that she had been drawing on earlier.

Musa's eyes lit up. "Hmm … that's not a bad idea. Let me try it!" Musa picked up the pencil and paper, and waved goodbye.

"Perhaps I'll go to Mrs. Juma's place first," Musa thought. Mrs. Juma was the lady who ran the local hair salon. Musa found her there, with her baby Daudi asleep on her back, finishing up some braids on a customer.

"Mama Daudi, may I draw you a picture?" Musa asked.

"Oh, Musa, how nice of you," said Mrs. Juma, "but do you expect to get paid?"

"Just a shilling," replied Musa.

Mrs. Juma paused, then said, "Well, maybe I could spare fifty cents. Want to do it?"

"*Sawa sawa*, madam, you got a deal!"

She posed and carefully, so carefully, Musa drew a picture of her.

"Musa," she said as he gave it to her, "that is very nice". She then dug into her purse and removed two small coins, "You know what, I just found another fifty cents. So that makes one shilling. Here you are." Musa could not believe it! He thanked her, and then stepped off to see who else would like a drawing.

Trotting along the beach, Musa spotted Bubu the fisherman putting away his nets and decided to ask him.

"Hello, Mr. Bubu. I was wondering if you would like me to draw a picture for you. I charge one shilling only," said Musa.

Bubu looked at him in surprise. "So, you are an artist, Musa? But how do I know that you are good? Will it be worth my shilling?"

"Yes, for sure! I drew a picture for Mrs. Juma just now and she liked it very much," Musa replied. "And … if you don't like it you don't have to pay for it."

"Well, hmm … okay. But make it nice, eh?" Bubu said.

Confidently, Musa drew the best that he could. Soon, a rather wonderful picture appeared.

"Musa … that is so nice! In fact, I think I will put it on my wall. Good job! Here's the shilling," Bubu said and handed Musa a coin.

"*Asante sana*, Mr Bubu," Musa said to thank him, and went on his way.

Mzee Omar owned a big hotel and Musa thought to ask him, for he must have money. Musa knocked on the door of the large two-story building.

After a few moments, that seemed more like a few hours, the door flew open. "*Kijana*, what do you want?" the huge, old man snapped.

"Sir, please let me draw a picture of you," Musa said politely.

"Ah! I don't have time for silliness!" he said and began to close the door.

"Sir, please, I am very fast and very good. I'm just trying to raise a few shillings. If you don't like it you don't have to pay," Musa said quickly.

"Ah!" the old man grunted and then sat down. "Okay, but make it speedy!"

Musa instantly came up with yet another good-looking picture. But as he was finishing this new masterpiece, *Mzee* snatched it away and took one mean look at it. Musa was so scared! But, slowly, a smile appeared on the old man's face. "Very good, young man. I'll take it, here's two *bob*," he said and tossed Musa two shillings.

"Oh, thank you so much, sir! Oh, thank you, thank you..."

"Ok, that   is enough! Now get out of here!"

Musa skipped away realizing that he now had four shillings, even more than he needed to get a *maandazi*! "Time to feed!" Musa cried out, and dashed off towards Mama Milka's place.

The smell of fresh *maandazis* became stronger and stronger as Musa neared the shop. When he arrived, though, he found the place all locked up.

"*Haiya*, this is not good! The shop is closed already? I won't get my *maandazi* today, after all that hard work? Ah!" Musa slumped onto a nearby stool, whimpering to himself, "it is not fair." In the distance some faint footsteps could be heard.

It was Mama Milka coming up the path!

"Mama Milka, I'm so glad to see you! I thought that you were gone for the day. I've got the money to buy a *maandazi*," Musa cried.

Mama's eyes widened in surprise as Musa pushed three shillings into her hand. "Very good, my young friend. I knew you could do it. I just stepped out to get a few things for my last batch of your favourite treat. Let me make them now."

Musa helped out, and soon piping hot *maandazis* were ready.
Mama made him a special, extra big one.
It was perfectly golden brown.

"Mmm! It smells so good! *Asante sana*, Mama Milka," Musa said with delight.

"*Karibu*," she replied, and handed it to him.

Musa wrapped half of this enormous *maandazi* in a paper to give to little sister Shani later. Then he took one huge bite into the *maandazi* ... the most beautiful, sweetest and tastiest *maandazi* that he'd ever, ever had.

Map of Kenya

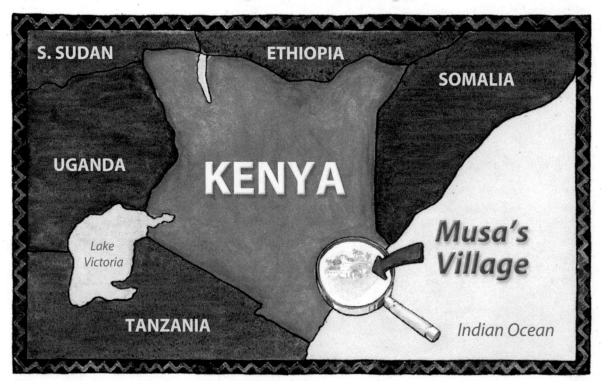

Swahili to English Dictionary

Asante = Thank you

Baba = Father

Bob = A nick-name for shilling, the name of the money used in Kenya

Haiya = An exclamation of surprise

Karibu = Welcome

Kijana = Young man, boy

Jambo = Greetings, hello

Lakini = But, however

Maandazi = A Kenyan deep-fried sweet bread, much like a donut

Mama = 1. Mother 2. Mother of (as in Mama Daudi, mother of Daudi)

Mzee = A term of respect for an old man

Sana = Very much

Sawa sawa = Okay, no problem

Mama Milka's Maandazi Recipe

Ingredients

2 eggs
1 cup of milk
1/2 cup of sugar
3 tablespoons of butter (or margarine)
1/2 teaspoon of ginger
1/2 teaspoon of cinnamon
1/4 teaspoon of cloves
3 and 1/2 cups of self-rising flour (or use 1 teaspoon of baking powder with ordinary flour)

Directions

1. Mix eggs and milk together in a bowl.
2. Mix flour, ginger, cinnamon and sugar together in a separate bowl.
3. Mix the wet and dry ingredients together.
4. Melt the butter and pour into the mixture.
5. Heat a deep skillet with about 2 inches deep of vegetable oil, on high heat.
6. Drop portions of the dough of about 1/4 cup into the hot oil and fry until golden brown. This portion size can vary according to the size of maandazi desired.

Serve warm!

Makes about 20 maandazis depending on the sizes created.

65209891R00024